Alison's Ghosts

Alison's Ghosts

by

Mary Alice Downie

& John Downie

James Lorimer & Company Ltd., Publishers
Toronto

James Lorimer & Company Ltd. acknowledges the support of the
Ontario Arts Council. We acknowledge the support of the Government
of Canada through the Book Publishing Industry Development
Program (BPIDP) for our publishing activities. We acknowledge the
support of the Canada Council for the Arts for our publishing program.
We acknowledge the support of the Government of Ontario through
the Ontario Media Development Corporation's Ontario Book
Initiative.

Cover design: Meghan Collins

The Canada Council | Le Conseil des Arts
for the Arts | du Canada

ONTARIO ARTS COUNCIL
CONSEIL DES ARTS DE L'ONTARIO

Library and Archives Canada Cataloguing in Publication

Downie, Mary Alice, 1934-

    Alison's ghosts / Mary Alice Downie and John Downie.

(Streetlights)

Originally published: Toronto: Nelson Canada, 1984.

ISBN 978-1-55277-013-9

    I. Downie, John II. Title. III. Series.

PS8557.O85A64 2008   jC813'.54   C2007-907512-6

James Lorimer & Company Ltd.,
Publishers
317 Adelaide Street West
Suite#1002
Toronto, Ontario, M5V 1P9
www.lorimer.ca

Distributed in the
United States by:
Orca Book Publishers
P.O. Box 468
Custer, WA U.S.A.
98240-0468

Printed and bound in Canada.

For Jack, who has a special magic of his own

1

Starry, Starry Night

"Where's Katie?" Alison scanned the crowd. She couldn't see her little sister anywhere. Well, she wasn't going to look for her and lose her place near the door.

"She's sitting in the shade," said Jill. "I told her to stay there until the doors open."

Alison Grant and her younger sisters, Jill and Katie, had been waiting outside the church for half an hour. The crowd was growing steadily. The heat of the day was still in the air. Soft dust from the road swirled around their feet.

"So, what are you going to buy?" Alison asked.

"Golf clubs!" said Jill. "I bet I can get an old set for five dollars."

Alison wasn't so sure, but she knew better than to argue with this sister. Although Jill was two years younger, she seemed to find a way to win any argument. Maybe it was because she was the middle sister and had to protect herself in two directions. Besides, no one ever knew what would turn up at the annual Starry, Starry Night Sale. Every summer, the people in their little Nova Scotia town collected their junk, then sold it back to each other to raise money for good causes. Early in the morning on the second Saturday in August, they began to set up tables in the United Church basement. It took them all day to arrange and put price tags on things before the crowd was allowed in that night.

"Hi, guys," said Katie. She ran up to them, just as the doors opened and everyone began to crowd through.

"Let's go," said Jill. The three girls were swept down the basement stairs in the flood of eager customers. Alison's sisters headed straight for the toy table while she wandered past battered chairs and stoves, tables stacked high with books and videos, piles of old *National Geographic* magazines and out-of-date computer manuals.

Alison saw her mother heading through the crowd toward her.

"There you are," she said, her face flushed with excitement. "Look what Grandma and I just found." She clutched an orange sundress with ruffles. "Do you think this would suit Jill?"

Alison made a face. "Maybe not ... " her mother said, and went back to try again.

This part of the church basement was full of hopeful mothers with heaps of soon-to-be-rejected clothes in their arms. A few tables over, Alison saw Jill racing along with a fishing pole and an armload of books. Katie trailed behind, pulling a quacking plastic duck on a string. Alison moved on to the Hidden Treasures table, which always had the best things. Captain Entwhistle, with his navy blue cap on the back of his head, was busy behind the table. He was in charge of it every year.

"Now, Mrs. McGregor," he boomed. "This brass bell from India will be just the thing for calling your grandchildren up from the shore."

"No, thank you," she said. "It might make them think they're back in school. They'll run away and hide!"

Alison inspected the rest of the table. There was a jumble of bells, boxes, and crates, and an old tin box full of brass buttons. At the far end, a row of cups that had lost their saucers were lined up opposite a pile of saucers without cups.

"Poor things," Alison said. "They look lonely." She could sympathize, because she often felt lonely herself, despite having two sisters and a bunch of cousins. Two of the cousins — James and Graham — were arriving the next day for the rest of the summer.

"What's that?" Captain Entwhistle asked. He was friendly and always willing to talk. Alison didn't want to hurt his feelings.

"Nothing," she said hastily. "I'm just looking."

"Here's a beauty." He rifled through a box of old spoons. "A present from Saint John, New Brunswick. You can see the Reversing Falls on the handle, and it's only three dollars.

What a bargain!"

"It sure is," Alison said politely. "But I don't have three dollars. What do you have for a toonie?"

"Try right there, my dear," said the Captain, pointing to the far side of the table. "Nothing above a loonie, and every one a treasure. I gathered these things from the four corners of the earth. But I must get back to my bells. Some day you must remind me to tell you about a religious ceremony I attended in India. Amazing sight, twenty cobras in a row, swaying to the music of the bells."

Alison moved to the far side of the table and poked at some things in an old tobacco tin. There was a Swiss Army knife. *Maybe this will be a good birthday present for Dad*, she thought. But most of the blades were snapped off, and the screwdrivers were worn almost round, so maybe not.

What's this?

She picked up a dark grey stone about the size of an egg. There were scratches — no, designs — cut into the outside surface. The top of the stone had been hollowed out to form a black hole, and there was another very small hole on the side near the bottom. Alison closed her eyes and rolled the mystery object between her hands, enjoying the cool feeling of the old stone.

Suddenly she felt dizzy. The room began to whirl around as if she'd done too many cartwheels in gym class.

Alison opened her eyes and blinked. The room was totally dark.

Must be a power failure, she thought. It would be the third one this summer. But why was everyone being so quiet?

Slowly, her eyes adjusted to the gloom.

Oh!

The white-painted walls of the church basement had disappeared, and so had all the people. She was inside a framework of poles covered with sheets of birchbark that circled completely around her. A fire burned in the centre. Spirals of smoke drifted up through a hole in the roof.

It's like that wigwam we saw at the museum in Halifax during March Break, she thought, proud of herself for remembering. She'd been so interested that she had done a school project on the Mi'kmaq people who lived in Nova Scotia for centuries before her ancestors arrived.

But how did she get in here? And what was a Mi'kmaq wigwam doing in a church basement?

Adventures were exciting to read about or watch on television, but maybe they weren't so much fun in real life.

Cautiously, she took a step forward, her heart thumping. Something crunched beneath her feet. What had been a linoleum floor was now covered with fur robes, and underneath them there were branches of fir.

She rubbed her eyes. They stung from the smoke.

Crack!

The fire snapped, sending up a fountain of sparks. Alison leapt back. *Where am I?* She wished desperately that Jill was there. Even four-year-old Katie would be a comfort.

She heard a soft leathery sound just outside. A flap opened on the wall of the wigwam. A ray of sunlight cut through the darkness. Then something, or someone, blocked the light. Alison shook, trying not to cry out. *It's coming in!*

A man stooped through the opening, then straightened until he towered over her. His hair was dark, and his face was streaked with red and black. Feathers flared out from both sides of his head like the wings of a bird. A long cloak, made of many furs, trailed on the ground.

Alison was too frightened to scream. *Maybe he's an actor they've brought in, like the people at the Habitation near Annapolis Royal who walk around pretending to be from another time.*

The stranger stared at her for a moment, as if searching for someone, then walked silently across the furs and sat down facing the fire.

He held out his arm, motioning for her to sit. *Run!*

But Alison's legs would not obey her. She sat down, repeating to herself, *This is a bad dream. You'll wake up soon.* But the ground felt very real.

The man spoke a few words in a husky, deep voice. It was a language she'd never heard before.

Alison shook her head. *I don't understand.* He stared at her puzzled face for a moment, then picked up a twig and drew in the sand beside the fire. He pointed to the drawing, but still she couldn't understand. *What does he want? He must be a medicine man — a shaman*, she thought, looking at the porcupine quill medicine pouch that hung from his belt.

The stranger spoke again. He made signs and puffing sounds. Then he pointed back to the drawing.

Of course!

Alison now saw that he had sketched a pipe — and the bowl was like the grey stone she held in her hand. She opened her fingers, looked at it, then placed it on top of the drawing.

"It fits!" she said, out loud. The man nodded and pointed to the long stem of the pipe in the drawing. He looked questioningly at her, but again, she shook her head.

"I don't have that part," she said. *I wish I did, then I could get out of here.*

The shaman began to speak, pointing at

Alison, then at the pipe stem, and at himself. His long finger repeated the pattern: Alison, the pipe stem, himself. Then he picked up the bowl of the pipe and placed it back in her hand.

"Well, young lady, do you think you should buy it?"

Suddenly Alison was back in the church basement. The tent, the smoke and the shaman had vanished as quickly as they had appeared. Once again the crowd milled around her. Captain Entwhistle was staring at her over his glasses.

"You feeling all right?" he asked. "You look a bit pale. Must be the heat in here. Why don't you sit down a minute and I'll rustle up a cold drink for you."

"I'm fine," Alison managed to say, although her hand shook when she put the stone back on the Treasure table. "Do you have the other part of the pipe?"

"So you recognized it, eh? That's clever. Not many people would," said Captain Entwhistle. "No, my dear, I don't have the stem. I found the bowl one day when I was looking around the old

Mackenzie place, but I couldn't find the rest. Funny, I don't even know how the bowl got into the box. I thought I'd lost it."

"Where's the old Mackenzie place?" Alison asked.

But another customer was waiting and was getting impatient.

"Take the pipe bowl, my dear," said the Captain, handing the stone to Alison. "Don't worry about paying me. We'll call it a present. Now you run along and get that cold drink." Then he turned away and began to sell yet another bell for taming cobras and calling back children.

2

Cousins

Alison wandered restlessly around the church basement until the Starry, Starry Night Sale was almost over. She felt confused and uneasy. *What had happened to her? Is there such a thing as a bad daydream? Could it be some kind of crazy magic?* She had never heard of anything like this happening in Nova Scotia.

Most of the people had left. The volunteers were joyfully counting their money and selling each other leftovers for a penny. Grandma was still shopping — she always liked to stay to the very end to look for last-minute bargains. Alison and her mother waited patiently as Grandma haggled over the price of a bowl that looked as if it had been made by a colour-blind potter. Katie busily arranged her plastic duck and three new dolls into a circle.

"What did you get?" Jill asked, walking up. "There weren't any golf clubs, but I found this." She proudly swished a warped tennis racket through the air, startling a mosquito.

"That's nice," said Alison, distracted. "I didn't get anything much." She felt Captain Entwhistle's gift deep inside her pocket. She didn't feel like explaining. She wouldn't have known how. She could still smell smoke and see the firelight reflected on the Mi'kmaq shaman's face. She needed some time to think about it.

The Grants left the church and headed for home. A cool wind from the bay rustled the trees. The sky was black and star-studded. Jill and Katie argued about who had the rights to a torn comic book, while Grandma and Mother gloated over their trophies and Alison thought about hers. *It must have been a dream. But how could it have been? I only dream when I'm asleep.* She fingered the stone in her pocket. The man or shaman or whatever he was, wanted the pipe stem, too. But why? What would have happened if she'd had the whole pipe? She shivered and grabbed Katie's sticky little hand for comfort.

They were now approaching Main Street, the centre of the town. The front porches of the neat frame houses cast twisted shadows on the lawns. A single lamppost lit the flowerbeds by the town hall and turned the pink petunias an eerie yellow. Alison shivered.

"Beat you home!" cried Jill who then tore off along the sidewalk. Katie trotted after her.

"Watch out for cars!" called their mother. Alison stayed behind with the grown-ups. She felt much better when they turned the corner and saw their old house with its welcoming light in the window.

The Grants' summer place was a rambling white house with bow windows, green gables, turrets and a widow's walk. It had been in their family for 150 years. Great-great-grandfather Grant, a sea captain like Captain Entwhistle, had built it after he retired.

When they got home, Grandma made hot chocolate, one of their favourite treats. Jill and Katie played in the living room with their new-old toys and books. The bargain clothes that their mother had found remained on the floor in a pile.

Alison took her mug upstairs to her bedroom to be alone and think. Pulling the pipe bowl from her pocket, she turned it slowly under her lamp, studying it carefully. It just looked like an ordinary grey stone with a hole in it.

She felt oddly disappointed. Summer holidays were lots of fun, especially since her cousins from Ontario were arriving tomorrow. But magic adventures, even scary ones, would certainly make things more interesting. *I'll tell James about it, anyway. He's ten and old enough to be sensible.*

Alison hid the pipe under her pillow for safe-keeping from nosy sisters, climbed into bed and fell asleep.

Dreams swirled through her head all night, scary dark dreams full of fire and smoke on stormy waves, shutters banging in the wind and a chilling, frightening fog.

Oh! Alison groaned as she woke up. She felt like crying. Bits of her nightmares stayed in her mind, but she couldn't remember them well enough to make herself feel better by describing them to her family at breakfast.

But there was no time to worry about bad dreams or wigwams appearing in church basements. Everyone was busy helping clean the house before the cousins came. Alison's job was to vacuum the bedrooms, and gather up all the seashells that Katie collected and hid around the house in unexpected places — like a small squirrel with a batch of nuts.

Jill went for the mail on an old bike, followed by Katie on foot roaring, "Wait for me!"

"I'm riding as slowly as I can, you snail," Jill called, pedalling faster.

"I'm not a 'nail!"

As Katie's voice faded down the road, Alison went in to make her bed. She was 'helped' by Grimble, a jaunty black and white kitten with a ruff under his neck that made him look like a clown. Although Grimble was very affectionate, he had one big fault. He couldn't resist nipping toes. Since everyone wore sandals most of the time, he had many temptations.

She lifted him off the bed and pulled up the blankets. He jumped on again, darted under the sheet and slithered along like a small purring sea serpent. He poked his head under the pillow, discovered the pipe, sniffed it suspiciously and began to pat it with his velvety paw.

"No you don't," Alison snatched the stone from the kitten and stuck it in her pocket. She knew he'd enjoy playing with it, but then Katie or Jill might find it. If the pipe really was magic, they could end up in a smoke-filled wigwam with a strange fur-cloaked man. *They'd have nightmares forever!* Then Alison thought about her sisters. *Maybe it'd be the shaman who'd have the nightmares!*

"They're here! They're here!"

Alison heard Grandma's excited cry and the chug-chug of an aging Volvo. Pipes and dreams forgotten, Alison ran out to the front steps with Grimble bounding and batting playfully at her heels.

Aunt Karin shut off the engine as the boys spilled out of the car. James and Graham let themselves be hugged by Grandma. Then they just stood and stared at Alison. She stared back. She hadn't seen her cousins since last summer.

They looked the same, only taller. Both boys were blond and skinny. James was the serious one. He read all the time and had a mind filled with useless facts, which he liked to share. He and Alison always argued. He thought he was better because he was a boy. She thought she was better because she was a year and two months and five days older. And she was a girl. But most of the time they were good friends.

"Where's Jill?" James asked coldly. Then he saw Grimble leaping by after a bee. He smiled and chased the kitten, suddenly looking like the James she remembered.

"Here she comes," Mother said. "Look."

They turned to see Jill pedalling so frantically up the road that the bicycle looked ready to fly apart. She had a box of cereal under one arm and a loaf of homemade bread from Mrs. MacLeod's bakery counter wedged under her chin. The newspaper was clenched between her teeth. Clouds of dust rose behind her.

Everyone laughed, especially when they saw Katie in the middle of the biggest cloud and heard her crying, "Wait for me!"

The cousins left the grown-ups to gossip and drink tea around the big kitchen table while they went out to the garden and sprawled on the grass. Grimble came too and began to scour Katie's dusty feet with his rough pink tongue.

"How was school?" Alison asked, trying to start a conversation.

"OK," said James. "When can we go swimming?"

"This afternoon," Jill said.

"I'm coming too." Katie was always afraid of being left behind because she was only four.

This is no fun, Alison thought. *We all seem so polite, like strangers.* "What do you want to do now?" she asked.

"Go to the wharf," said James.

"To the store for ice cream cones," said Jill.

"To the fishing shacks," answered Graham.

"To the swings," said Katie.

Everybody laughed, and suddenly it was all right. The five cousins ran off together down the sunlit street.

3

The Haunted House

During the next few days the cousins had a glorious time. They rode all over the place on the family collection of rickety bikes. They went swimming every day, even in the fog. They built magnificent sand castles with moats and walls, seaweed banners and tiny crabs from the tidal pools as guards. And almost every night they went down to the shore to watch the sunset and play freeze tag in the fading light.

If it weren't for the dreams, everything would be perfect.

Alison had been dreaming almost every night. Flashes of birchbark, crackling flames, someone in a cloak of furs with a sad face.

"I can hear you at night all the way from my room," Jill complained after breakfast one day. "You keep making whimpering noises in your sleep." The cousins were all sitting at the dining room table trying to see who could eat the most toast and blueberry jam.

"No I don't," Alison said.

"You do too," said Katie.

"What's bugging you, anyway?" Jill asked.

"A guilty conscience," James suggested, looking wise.

"No, it's not a guilty conscience." Alison hesitated. They had been so busy having fun that she hadn't told anyone in the family about the pipe and what had happened at the Starry, Starry Night Sale. The dark wigwam and the Mi'kmaq shaman just seemed too weird to think about now with her cousins here. Besides, Alison was afraid that they might laugh at her.

But maybe now's the time.

She took a deep breath and pulled the stone from her pocket. "I think it's because of this." She set her hidden treasure on the table. "Captain

Entwhistle gave it to me at the sale."

Three blond heads and a small red one bent over the stone, studying it while Alison told her story. There was a long silence when she finished.

Finally, James spoke. "It must have been a dream."

"I sure hope it was a dream," Graham said.

"Me too," said Alison.

"Do you think the shaman wanted the bowl?" Jill picked it up and tried to blow it like a whistle.

"If he did, why didn't he keep it right then?" James asked.

"I think he wanted the whole pipe," Alison replied. "I think I'm supposed to find it for him. But I don't know where to look, or how to give it back to him if I do find it."

"Give him one of Daddy's pipes instead," Katie said. They all laughed and suddenly Alison felt much better.

"Maybe Captain Entwhistle has the stem," Jill suggested.

"I don't think so. He said he found just the bowl in some old house called the Mackenzie place."

"I know the Mackenzie place." They all turned and stared at James.

"How?"

"Where is it?"

"Dad told me last summer. It's the haunted house down by the shore."

Quickly, Alison put the stone back into her pocket. Jill's face was very serious. Every kid in town knew about the haunted house. It stood grey and deserted on the far side of town. Even the bravest avoided it, and not just at Halloween.

"What would a Mi'kmaq pipe be doing in that old house?" asked Jill.

"Maybe it's built on a place where they camped long ago," James said.

"So, who wants to go look for the stem at the haunted house?" Alison asked, hesitantly.

"I do," said Graham, popping up from behind an old armchair, clutching a cross and dusty Grimble.

"Good idea," said Jill. "The dishes can wait."

"No, they can't," said their mother, coming into the dining room, a tangle of cobwebs in her hair. She held up a pair of bright pink shorts. "Look what I found in the attic. Do you suppose they'll fit anyone?"

"Katie, you try them," Alison said quickly. She went out to the kitchen and began running the hot water. As they washed, dried and put away the dishes, they made plans to visit the haunted house at once.

"Can we have a picnic?" Graham asked, but his idea was ignored. Once the dishes were done, and Katie was settled in the garden with James's Lego set and the promise they would later build not one, not two, but three sandcastles, the cousins set off.

The tide was out, so they took the shore road. Mist rolled in from the bay as they crossed the sandbar. The foghorn mooed forlornly from the harbour like a homesick cow.

"Maybe we should have gone the long way," said Graham.

"We're almost there," said Alison.

They trudged along in silence. For some reason they began walking more and more slowly. *What might be waiting for them?* Alison wondered. *What magic? What danger?*

"Look, there it is!"

The old house stood lonely and abandoned on the bank ahead. It seemed to have grown out of the thick carpet of mist.

"Do you really think it's haunted?" Jill asked.

"I don't believe in ghosts," Alison said firmly.

"Well, we're not turning back now," said James as he climbed up the bank.

The house was surrounded by a tangle of wild roses, gooseberries, chokecherries and hazelnut trees. "An orchard," James said with the superior tone he used when sharing an important piece of misinformation. "That proves it was a Mi'kmaq campsite."

"Maybe we should go swimming instead." Graham sounded more like a mouse than the captain of his hockey team.

"Are you scared?" James gave him a sharp look.

"Of course he isn't," Jill said fiercely.

They walked up the overgrown path to the

house. The veranda had a lacy wood railing but large chunks had fallen away, leaving it with a toothless look. Honeysuckle vines twined around the wood pillars and an ancient lilac hovered over the rotting steps. The glass in the windows was either cracked or broken. Shutters hung at crazy angles, ready to fall at a sneeze.

"This house is like *Sleeping Beauty*," Alison whispered.

"Okay, each of us should hunt for the pipe stem in a different room," James proposed. "That way, if there is a ghost, someone will be sure to see it."

"I'll take the porch." Graham curled a scrawny arm around a cracked grey pillar, propped himself against the railing and refused to budge.

James was disgusted. "We should have known better than to bring an eight-year-old scaredy-cat. I'll take the attic. That's the most likely place for a ghost to be lurking." He pushed open the front door and disappeared into the gloom of the hall.

"I'll search the second floor." Jill's voice had a funny trembling sound to it.

Alison looked at her, concerned.

"Why don't you wait outside with Graham?" she suggested.

"No, I'm going in!" Jill tramped up the stairs, whistling loudly.

"That noise is enough to scare any ghost," said Graham as he picked splinters of wood and peeling paint from the pillar and dropped them into the bushes.

"I guess the main floor is left for me." Alison went slowly into the front hall. Long strips of faded, floral wallpaper drooped from the walls. She could hear Jill stomping about overhead, still whistling defiantly. James's footsteps faded entirely.

To her left was a large wooden door with a big crack and no door handle. She pushed it open and walked in. The room had once been the living room, she guessed. Now it was empty. Nothing but cobwebs, old nests and dust.

"Yuck!"

She stepped on something soft and squishy. She couldn't bear to look. Slowly, she moved her shoe sideways. *Ew!* It was a small dead bird, a sparrow.

Quickly, Alison went back into the hall. The door on the other side was missing. The dining room was empty, too, except for a large wooden cupboard built into one corner. The glass in the two doors was broken. Below them were two drawers, both of them closed.

That would be a good place to look.

She walked over to it, avoiding the broken pieces of glass all over the floor. There was nothing inside except an empty green bottle and more dust. She opened a drawer. It was empty. The second drawer didn't have a knob. Alison was just removing the top drawer to try to get at it when she heard rustling behind her. Without turning she said, "Jill? Come and help with this."

There was no answer.

"Jill?"

"Who are you?"

Alison spun around. A girl about her age stood there in a dark blue dress with white buttons down the front. The hem of her dress was looped up over a pair of old-fashioned boots. Her dress was different somehow, and so was her hair — long brown curls tied back with a ribbon.

"Who are you?" the girl repeated as she crossed the room and stood guarding the cupboard. "What are you looking for in here?"

"I'm not looking for anything!" Alison stopped, embarrassed. If this strange girl lived here, what right did she have to be poking around in her house? It was supposed to be empty. *Maybe her family is just moving in. They just haven't had time to clean the place.*

"My name is Lucia," the girl said. She nodded at Alison's denim cut-offs. "Why are you dressed like a boy?" Before Alison could answer, she continued: "Have you seen my father? Has he stopped at the tavern again?" She looked ready to cry.

"The tavern? There aren't any bars in this town," Alison said.

Lucia stared at her. "There's Ferguson's, down by the harbour. Papa never went there before Mama died, but now he does. We haven't any food left and I am so hungry."

Alison looked more closely at the girl's dress. It was patched. Her fear began to dissolve. "I-I-I'm sorry," she stuttered. "Here, I think I have a granola bar in my pocket."

"What is a granola bar?"

"Who are you talking to?"

Alison turned. Jill stood, still and pale in the doorway. "Who are you talking to?" she repeated.

"Her name is Lucia. This is my sister … " But when Alison turned back, Lucia had vanished.

"Alison's seen a ghost!" Jill shrieked. She turned and ran out the front door.

Footsteps thundered down the stairs. "I'm out of here!" cried James as he raced outside and down the path. Shocked by their flight, Alison bolted, too. She flew out the door like a leaf on the wind, right past Graham, still sitting on the veranda.

"Hey, wait for me!" With a frightened glance at the house, Graham ran for his life.

4

The Children's Art Show

The four cousins ran all the way home and collapsed on the grass under the apple tree, gasping for breath.

"What's the matter, you guys?"

It was Katie, crawling around in the bushes after Grimble. There were leaves in her hair and mud was smeared across her face.

"That's enough of ghosts," said Alison, still red-faced from running. "Let's put that stupid pipe out in the barn until Dad comes. Then we can show it to him."

They all agreed and went with her to find a hiding spot. Alison tucked the pipe bowl safely under a dusty old flower pot, covered with spider webs. *That feels better already*, she thought as they came back into the sunlight.

"Time for popsicles!" cried Graham.

"Yeah!" Everyone felt the need to celebrate.

On the way to the store, they met Grandma struggling up the road with three large cardboard boxes.

"I've had a brainwave," she announced triumphantly.

The children exchanged glances. Grandma's brainwaves usually meant a lot of work, but they were always fun in the end.

"What is it?" Graham asked.

"Can we have another children's auction like we did last summer?" asked Jill.

"Great, we could sell James," said Graham. "But who would buy him?"

"We're going to have a children's art show," Grandma announced, ignoring the rude remark. "The municipal council wants to buy new benches and picnic tables for Centennial Park, and you children are going to help raise the money."

"I already know what I'm going to make," said James as he gallantly took two of Grandma's boxes.

"Thank you, dear," she said. "Now you must all bring more boxes when you come back from the store. We're going to need dozens."

All week long the cousins prepared for the art show. They scoured the village for large boxes and decorated them with old paint they found in the barn so that they looked like children's blocks. The paintings would be displayed on the sides of the box and the sculptures, wood carvings and decorated rocks would be placed on top.

Alison and Grandma made posters advertising the show:

Children's Art Show

Saturday at
The Old Schoolhouse
7:00 to 8:00 p.m.

Proceeds for the purchase of
new park benches and picnic tables.
Prizes. Fiddle Music. Punch.

Jill and Graham took the posters all over town on their bikes. They hung them on the notice board at the post office, at the town hall, and on all the doors and windows of the storekeepers on Main Street who had donated prizes.

Before they knew it, it was Friday — only one day left until the art show. Not one of the cousins had had time to work on an entry. It was a dull, drizzly morning. The foghorn moaned from the harbour as grey fog crept up from the shore.

"It's a perfect day for art," said Grandma, looking out the rain-streaked window. After breakfast dishes were done, the cousins gathered around the dining room table. Grandma set out rolls of shelf paper, crayons, pastels, water colours, modelling clay and lots of sequins, which were her favourites.

Jill started right away, drawing the lines for a patchwork quilt design. She always made her mind up quickly about these projects. Katie scrawled what she said was a picture of Grimble protecting a bird's nest. Then she crawled under-neath the table and began painting everyone's

41

toenails bright green. James frowned with concentration as he tried to mould a spaceship out of Plasticine. Graham worked on a drawing of a horse, but everyone said it looked like a dog.

Alison stared at the blank paper. She usually found it hard to get started. At last she had an idea. "I'm going to paint that big brass bowl filled with nasturtiums," she said, pointing to the bowl on the windowsill. Grandma had found it one year at an auction.

Alison dipped her paintbrush in the water, then on the little square of orange colour. She made a few quick strokes. Next, she chose yellow, and then green for the leaves. She washed out her brush and went to apply peach — then stopped.

It can't be!

The orange and the yellow and the green weren't there anymore. There was red paint on the paper! And black! Alison blinked and looked again. The flowers she had been drawing had disappeared.

Her beautiful painting had become a face — a dark, troubled face streaked with red and black.

42

Horrified, Alison tore up the painting before the others could see it. But they were too busy on their own art projects to notice. She began again. And again. No matter how much she tried, each time her cheerful flowers were transformed into the Mi'kmaq shaman's head.

Miserable and more and more afraid, she hesitated. *What if I stop trying to paint flowers? What will happen?* Sure enough, the brush now seemed to move her hand. The painting grew more vivid and haunted with each stroke as the shaman's face took shape and wild wings stuck out on either side of his head. "Help me!" it seemed to be saying. "Find the stem."

It's the stone, I know it. Even hidden in the barn, Alison had had an awful feeling that the old pipe bowl wasn't finished with her. Now she was sure of it. Although she hadn't said anything to her cousins about it over the last few days, her bad dreams had continued. And now they were more troubling than ever. She often saw Lucia standing in an empty room in her dark blue dress.

Even if Lucia were a ghost, Alison decided that she hadn't been really frightening. In fact, Alison wished she could have spoken with her longer. But they had all fled in a panic. Alison made up her mind. She'd look for the pipe stem and for Lucia. Maybe she could help her, although she didn't know how. She wasn't brave enough to go back to the old Mackenzie place yet, but some day soon she would. She looked into the eyes of the man in the painting. *I promise you, I will.*

She glanced around the table. Jill had moved on to a bigger and better drawing of her quilt design. James wrestled with his spaceship, which looked more like an elephant. Graham was making a knight to go on top of his horse.

"Cookies, anyone?"

Alison's mother came in from the kitchen carrying a plate of gingerbread still warm from the oven. She wandered around the table admiring the works of art while the artists tested her baking.

"That's a fine … "

"Horse," said Graham.

"Yes, a fine horse," she agreed, looking at it again.

She came to Alison's painting. "And what a splendid Mi'kmaq man! But why the troubled expression on his face? It's heartbreaking."

"It was supposed to be a bowl of flowers," Alison said, defiantly. "That one over there." She pointed to the nasturtiums on the window ledge.

Her mother looked from the man to the bouquet and back again. "Really?" she said, doubtfully.

Jill came over to see the painting. She turned on Alison. "You said no more scary stuff!"

"I couldn't help it. Anyway, it's just a picture." She didn't know how to explain it.

"Well, it's very good," Jill admitted as the others gathered around to look at it. "Maybe you'll even win a prize." But at that moment, Alison was too upset to care.

The next afternoon the cousins took their entries to the old schoolhouse.

"Off you go now," Grandma said after receiving their art projects at the door. "No children allowed

45

inside until tonight, not even family."

She turned back inside, gathering her volunteer helpers like a cheerful but determined general. Through the open door, the cousins watched Aunt Karin and several ladies from the village as they stacked the painted boxes into piles of blocks. Soon the judges would arrive to begin their work.

Alison's mother was in charge of the refreshments. When the children got back to the house, they found her in the kitchen pouring cold tea, cranberry juice, lemonade and ginger ale into a big blue cauldron. It was her special secret punch.

"Mmm, can we have some?" Katie asked.

"Of course," said their mother. "At the schoolhouse tonight."

After a quick hamburger supper, it was time to get dressed. Dresses and shirts felt very strange and uncomfortable to the children after so many days in T-shirts and cut-offs. They even wore shoes and socks, much to Grimble's annoyance.

When the cousins reached the old schoolhouse, they hardly recognized it. It had been transformed. The painted boxes had become cubes of blazing colour. Tall wicker baskets filled with lilies and mallows and cattails were arranged against the walls. Jimmy MacLeod, the best fiddler in the county, was tuning up on a small stage with his son and grandson — who were the second and third best.

The room was hot and noisy, jammed with artists and their parents, all hunting for their art entries and, hopefully, a ribbon that showed they had won a prize.

"Wicked!" Jill whooped with delight. She'd spotted her "Crazy Quilt" and the red ribbon beside it.

The others weren't so lucky. There was no ribbon beside James's spaceship. Katie had forgotten to hand in her drawing so, of course, there was no ribbon for her.

"Yes!" cried Graham. His knight on horseback had won an honourable mention. That was a blue ribbon.

At last, Alison spotted her Mi'kmaq shaman. Splendid, tortured, mysterious, he glared from the side of a purple cube. But there was no ribbon beside him. Although the painting had frightened her when she was making it, she was surprised at how disappointed she felt. She walked slowly over to the refreshments table where her mother was busy ladling out Pirate Punch with one hand and adding ice cubes with the other, to make it go further.

"It's a shame," her mother said, handing her a cup. "That's the best thing you've ever done. So dramatic, yet touching too. It should have won a ribbon. Everyone says so."

"Maybe if I'd stuck to flowers," Alison murmured. She took another cup of what was rapidly becoming Ice Cube Punch and went out to the front steps to cool off. The street was dark and empty. The swishing of the trees in the wind blended with the fiddle music from inside.

She heard a soft jingling. "That's quite a picture, my dear."

Captain Entwhistle stood beside her on the steps and placed a comforting hand on her shoulder. "If those judges are such nitwits that they can't see the talent in a picture like yours — " He reached inside his ancient jacket. "I'll give you an award of my own — for the most imaginative painting in the show." He produced a small carving of a whale. "It's soapstone, from the Arctic," he said.

"Thank you." Alison said, her spirits lifting a little. "I don't deserve it though." She hesitated. "The picture, it just seemed to paint itself. I was trying to paint flowers, but they kept changing, coming out as that face."

"You don't say!"

Captain Entwhistle didn't sound very surprised. "By the way, have you found a stem for that pipe yet?"

"No, I wanted to ask you. Do you have any idea where it could be?" Nice though the Captain was, she wasn't quite ready to tell him about their adventure at the haunted house. Maybe they'd been silly to run away.

"Funny place, that old house," he mused, as if he had read her mind. "The Mackenzies were kin of mine, you know. Yours, too, although you're connected on the other side through the MacGregors. Kinzie Mackenzie's Aunt Lizzie was my grandmother's … " Captain Entwhistle drifted off on a gentle tide of family memories.

Alison was no longer surprised to learn about unexpected cousins. They kept turning up all the time. One way or another, she and Jill suspected that they were related to almost everyone in the county. "The pipe stem," she reminded the Captain politely. "Where should I look for it?"

Captain Entwhistle returned from his ancestor-hunting. "Ah, yes. There were some strange stories about that pipe, my dear."

"Do you remember them?"

Captain Entwhistle frowned, his voice grew serious. "Dark tales they were of grief and sadness, lonely wanderings throughout the years."

That wasn't much help. "Do you have any ideas?" Alison asked, hoping for something more useful.

"To find something," the Captain said, "you only have to believe it exists." He seemed to be seeing something far away and long ago. "Then

be prepared to spend a lifetime looking for it."
He patted her shoulder. "There, there, I shouldn't
tease, my dear. I have no idea where you'd find the
stem." He paused and thought for a moment.
"I'm not so sure that you should look for it after
all. But if you do come across it, let me know."

"Then none of the stories are true?" Alison
asked, crushed.

"Oh, we're all distantly related. And there
were some strange tales told in my mother's day
about the old house and its last owners. But I
really don't know how much truth there is in
them."

Alison followed Captain Entwhistle back into
the crowd of artists and proud parents. "I'm
going to look everywhere until I find that stem,"
she said.

"Well, be careful," he cautioned her as they
headed toward the punch bowl. "I want to be the
first to know if you do. Don't forget."

5

Swallows

Alison was in no mood for hunting pipe stems the next morning. The whole family felt like grinches. Katie had had nightmares and woke everyone except Jill with her moans. Then at four in the morning, Grimble had climbed up the honeysuckle vine to Grandma's bedroom where he meowed and clawed at the window until she let him in. There had been thunder and pounding rain, too. Nobody got much sleep.

"We were all just overexcited." Mother buttered a piece of toast as if it were her worst enemy.

"It's the post-art show blues," Grandma said cheerfully to the scowling faces around the breakfast table.

"What are you going to do today, children?" Aunt Karin asked, trying to make peace.

"Fight!" replied James. And that's just what they did, until their mothers separated them and made everyone apologize to everyone.

"Why don't you all go down and get the news-paper?" suggested Aunt Karin.

"And the mail," added Grandma.

"And don't hurry back!" Mother called as they tromped out of the house.

The trees along the road dripped on the cousins' heads. Long wet blades of grass soaked their running shoes and socks and feet. A straggly gull hovered overhead, shrieking at a hawk, and then vanished in the rain and mist.

Grimble had started to follow them, but changed his mind and hid under the porch, growling quietly.

"Let's be ducks!" Graham stepped into a puddle, quacked loudly and splashed James with cold water.

"Cut it out!" James yelled, splashing his brother back, and making him even wetter.

When they reached the post office, there was no mail except a telephone bill for Grandpa. And all the butter tarts and bread and newspapers were sold out. It was that kind of day.

Luckily for everyone, Grandma had another idea when they padded grumpily into the living room, leaving a trail of muddy footprints on the floor.

"You're all going to Mr. Cinders' farm," she announced. "And while you're gone, Katie and I will have a lovely time baking gingersnaps."

Maybe I can find the missing pipe stem there! Alison thought.

Until he had retired to his farm, Mr. Cinders had owned one of the best antique stores in the area. His customers never knew what they'd find: a wicker rocker, the model of a Bluenose schooner or a carved duck decoy. Mr. Cinders had taken all his leftover stock to the farm with him and was still open to visitors once in a while.

Alison slipped away to the barn to get the pipe bowl. She decided not to mention it to anyone. They were already mad enough at her.

It didn't take long to reach Mr. Cinders' farm. He lived in an enormous yellow house with gables and two copper weathervanes on the peaked roof. When they drove up, a black and white sheepdog burst from the house and ran barking around the car as if it were a stray sheep he had to herd.

"Morning, folks."

Mr. Cinders came down the steps smiling, which was lucky. Some days, when he was in a bad mood, he would tell customers he was closed.

"Yup, it's a good day for antiquing." Talking all the way, Mr. Cinders led them to the huge barn where he kept his treasures. The sun came out just as they reached the doorway. It seemed like a good omen.

The front part of the barn was jam-packed with furniture, quilts and china. There was even an old pump organ. Aunt Karin sat down immediately and began to play. Jill found a laundry basket filled with promising junk. James pounced on an almost-new soccer ball and Graham discovered a box of ancient bottles, including one with red ink in it.

Alison was sure she would find the other half of the pipe. She waited patiently for Jill to finish digging through the basket, and then picked her way through the stuff three times. But there was no stem.

She wandered after her mother and Aunt Karin who had gone into the back part of the barn. The rest of the gang had found a pile of old comic books and sat with their noses buried in tales of superheroes.

The back room was far more interesting. *Like a barn should be*, she thought. It was filled with faded red or green painted sleighs, cutters, old farm machinery and wagons. Ancient fishing rods, hip waders, nets and wicker creels for holding fish were piled in one corner all covered with a mousy coat of dust. Swallows circled overhead, darting through the high open windows near the roof.

Alison sat on a wooden milking stool and leaned against a bale of hay. She watched her mother and Aunt Karin, their faces streaked with dirt, as they rooted among boxes filled with oil lamps, bottles and crocks.

Putting her hand in her pocket, Alison's fingers closed around the mysterious stone. *I'll never find that stem here. There's way too much stuff.*

If I were a bird, I'd fly all over this barn hunting for it. Then maybe …

Suddenly she felt dizzy, light-headed, almost as if she were fluttering upwards through the air. She looked down.

Oh! The floor was a metre below her, then two, as Alison went higher and higher, up to the roof. She was flying!

Sometimes she had dreams where she was flying, but this felt real, exciting and frightening at the same time!

Yikes!

Down she plummeted toward the ground. Instinctively, Alison stuck out her arms, flailing at the air. It worked. She stopped falling. Awkwardly, Alison tried flapping her arms — *wings!* She went higher, a little unsteadily, but she was going up.

This is amazing.

She flew up into the cobwebbed rafters and

landed, breathing hard, exhilarated. Then she noticed an untidy nest made mostly of mud with several odd-looking twigs sticking out of it.

Should I? She stepped off the rafter and flew over to look at the nest. But there was no pipe stem among the sticks.

"Hey, look at me, everyone. I'm flying!"

Her mother and Aunt Karin didn't even look up. *They can't hear me!*

Strangely, Alison didn't mind for the moment. Instead, she fluttered back and forth across the barn, checking out nests, dusty corners and faded old boxes stored high up on piles. Nothing there. But the flying was fun. She swooped, twisted and turned, did loop-the-loops, chased several friendly swallows in circles. As they whizzed past an owl drowsing on a rafter, it opened its great yellow eyes and glared at them. *It could have me for lunch. Yuck.*

Alison decided she'd been a bird long enough. But she had no idea how to change back to her regular self. She called to her Mother, to Aunt Karin below, but all that came out were a series of chirps.

"Aren't the birds in the country noisy when there aren't any cars to drown them out," her mother said, her voice sounding tiny and far away.

No, it's me, Mother! Can't you see?

"We'd better be off," her mother said. "The children will be getting restless."

"Help!" Alison cried. "Save me! I don't want to be a bird forever." She flew down and perched, in a wobbly way, on the milking stool. Surely her own mother would recognize her!

But she didn't even notice. She was talking with Aunt Karin, holding a pile of old blue dinner plates. She started to put them down on the stool.

No! Don't!

The plates loomed like a dangerous blue cloud over Alison's head. She skittered across the top of the stool, chirping wildly, then slid over the edge and landed with a thump.

"Hey, you guys, look at this! Alison was sleeping and fell off the stool."

Alison looked up into Jill's laughing face.

I'm a girl again.

"Come on, sleepyhead, we've been looking for

you," said James. "Everyone's ready to go." He held out his hand and pulled his cousin to her feet. "Did you have any good dreams this time?"

Alison brushed off the hay and dust, trying to hide her embarrassment. "Everyone dozes off sometimes," she muttered.

"But not everyone falls off chairs," said James, laughing. "That takes talent."

Alison didn't talk much on the way home. *That was definitely not a dream*, she told herself. *And I sure didn't dream up Lucia.* The others had all felt *something* in the haunted house, even if they wouldn't admit that they saw anything. There was only one way to find out.

I'm going back to that house. If the others won't come, I'll go by myself.

6

Lucia

It was one thing for Alison to bravely plan a visit alone to the haunted house while sitting in a car with her chattering relatives. It was quite a different thing to set off by herself. During the next few days, she kept finding excellent reasons for staying close to home.

The lazy golden days of August were upon the family. They spent long sunny afternoons at the shore, plunging into the cold water and then chasing each other to warm up. When it eventually rained, Aunt Karin took James and Graham into town to Frenchy's to buy almost-new clothes for school. *School* was a word they all dreaded. It meant summer was ending.

Alison and her sisters stayed home. Their mother didn't believe in special outfits for the first day of school, except maybe for new white socks, which you can get any time. Alison and Jill moped around the house while Grandma, their mother and Katie took afternoon naps. The two sisters finally settled down in Alison's bedroom.

Jill had Katie's markers and was busy colouring in her sketchbook. Alison opened *How Glooskap Made the Birds and Other Tales*, a book of legends she was supposed to read for a summer book report — which she'd kept putting off.

Alison couldn't stop thinking about the mysterious pipe. She put the book down. It couldn't have been just a dream, but there wasn't much time left to prove it. And once her dad and Grandpa and Uncle Bruce arrived for the rest of their holidays, the days would zip by and before she knew it, she'd be back at school.

Alison finally admitted to herself that she didn't want to go to the haunted house alone. It was just too frightening. She glanced at Jill, who lay sprawled on the bed, a smudge of purple marker on her nose.

"I think the old Mackenzie place has something to do with the pipe," she said.

"No pipes, no haunted houses." Jill set her jaw in the stubborn way that meant she wouldn't be budged by anyone. "You promised to forget it until Dad comes, remember?"

"I know, but what if it's all a silly mistake? Suppose I dreamed the whole thing? Wouldn't it be better to check the house once more? Then I'll know for sure if it was just a dream."

"What do you expect to find?" Jill asked. "We all looked for that stupid pipe stem and it wasn't there. There's nothing in that creepy place except a dead bird and a bunch of spiders and starving moths."

"I don't know. I just … I saw a girl. At least I think I saw a girl," Alison added quickly when she saw Jill's darkening face. "I need to go again. Just come with me. Please!"

"No way." Jill returned to her colouring book, trying to ignore her.

"I'll set the table for you for a whole month."

"Forget it."

"*And* I'll make your bed for a month, too."

Jill looked at her sister. "Promise?"

"Promise."

"Well, okay," said Jill, reluctantly. "But I'm not going inside!"

"We'll take my watch," Alison said. *And the pipe.* "If I'm not out in ten minutes you can call me. Anyway, it's better than sitting around yawning at home."

Jill was still unconvinced.

"Let's go."

They trudged through the fog and mist in silence. Alison had planned to bring a picnic lunch for Lucia as a treat, but had decided against it in the end. All the books she'd taken out of the town library that summer said ghosts don't eat.

The girls reached the abandoned house, now looking more lonely than ever. The lilac leaves were faded and shrivelled. Rotting chokecherries carpeted the path.

Alison handed her watch to Jill. "If I'm not back in half an hour, you start calling."

"What if something *else* answers?" Jill asked gloomily.

Alison went inside, leaving her sister hunting for a dry spot on the leaky porch.

The hall was cold and empty. Little feet scurried inside the walls. *Squirrels*, she told herself fiercely.

Creak.

Loose floorboards groaned as she stepped toward the living room. Slowly, cautiously, she opened the door and crept into the room.

Instantly, the atmosphere of the house changed. It felt lived-in and warm. In the dim light Alison could see wood and glass and copper glinting in the light from the fireplace.

It's full of furniture! A deep shiver shook Alison down to her toes.

"Oh!" There was someone hunched in a rocking chair beside the stove, a man. *He heard me.* But the person paid no attention.

"E-e-excuse me," Alison said weakly. The man continued to ignore her.

Goodness, can't they hear my heart pounding?

Alison walked slowly across the room. And then she saw her. The man in the rocking chair was talking to a young girl seated on the floor beside him.

"Lucia," Alison whispered. She didn't want to startle her. But the girl didn't seem to hear her either. She turned her head to speak to the man, and looked straight at Alison — and right through her!

Alison crept closer still, until she stood right beside them. Funny, she could feel the warmth of the fire, but to Lucia and the man she was invisible.

Now I'm the ghost, she said to herself. *A ghost from the future!*

"And so you see," the man said to Lucia in a low voice, "although I can't explain it, I feel that all our misfortunes are somehow connected to this pipe. I've never said that to anyone else, of course. They'd think I'd lost my mind." He looked down, and Alison saw that he held the whole pipe in his hand. She felt in her pocket, and the bowl was gone.

It must have travelled back to be with the stem!

"Ever since I got it, misery has plagued us. Your mother died last year, though she'd always been a healthy woman. And this year, the harvest was poor again. I don't know how we'll survive the winter."

"Can't you get rid of the pipe, Father?" Lucia asked.

"I've tried to destroy it," he replied, "but I can't. I've tried to lose it, but it always reappears. I thought of giving it away, but if I'm right about its strange powers, then how in good conscience could I give it to anyone?"

"Who gave it to you?"

"A poor wanderer stopped at the farm one day. He was starving and I gave him some bread and cheese. He wanted to give me the pipe in return for the food. At first I refused, but he insisted. I remember that he said a strange thing: 'Perhaps if it is exchanged for a good deed, we may both prosper.' Untruer words were never spoken. I've had nothing but bad luck ever since."

"Why don't you just throw it into the stove?" asked Lucia.

Her father smiled sadly. "I tried that. I don't believe in magic or spirits, so when I first experienced this feeling of dread, I told myself I was a fool and tossed the pipe into the fire. That night I became ill, burning with fever until dawn and then shaking with cold. The stove went out. I dragged myself over to light it and get some warmth in my bones. There in the cold ashes lay the entire pipe. The wooden stem hadn't been destroyed in the flames. It wasn't even singed!"

Lucia's father stared at the pipe as he spoke, turning it slowly in his hands. Then he removed the bowl and laid it on the small table beside him while he cleaned the long stem. "Life here is hard," he said to his daughter. "Every family has its troubles. Perhaps ours are harder to bear because they have come so suddenly. This old pipe is only a piece of stone and wood after all, but I'd like to be free of it just the same."

Alison looked from one sad face to the other, and then at the pipe bowl lying on the small twig table. She wanted to do something to help, but what? *Maybe if I took it*, she told herself. She reached out, picked up the bowl and put it in her pocket. Then, slowly she backed away from them into the shadows as Lucia's father sat staring into the flames.

He sighed and reached for the bowl to put the pipe together again. "Where has it gone?" He looked in surprise at the empty table.

Lucia's father looked around on the floor and then under his chair. "That's strange. All my talk of trying to get rid of this pipe, and now I can't find half of it when I know I put it on this table only a moment ago."

Lucia and her father searched everywhere. "How odd," he kept muttering as they searched the chairs and cabinets and bookshelves in the room.

Suddenly he stopped. "Lucia! Get your mother's bag. Pack whatever you value most. Take what food we have and put it into a sack. For some strange reason, I have a feeling of being free, of a chance to begin again. We'll leave this cursed place behind and find a new life in Upper Canada."

The man looked much younger as he moved quickly around the room, collecting items to pack. He even started to hum a tune. Alison could hardly believe he was the same person.

"Can we really leave, Father?" asked Lucia, doubt and surprise in her voice.

He smiled and nodded. "I don't know why we didn't go long ago. I have hated this house ever since your dear mother died."

"Leave the stem, Father," Lucia begged. "I'm afraid of it. Hide it somewhere."

"All right, my dear," he said cheerfully. Alison could hardly believe he was the same person. "My father used to say, 'If you want to hide a tree, put it in a forest.'"

He picked up a little table beside the fire, made from criss-crossed and twisted branches. He slid the stem in among the bent twigs until it looked like one of them.

Then Lucia and her father brushed past Alison, looking right through her as they rushed through the house.

Alison waited, listening to them upstairs and then back down in the kitchen. Before long, they were in the hall.

A whistle sounded from outside the house.

Lucia and her father seemed not to notice. With a last glance around the living room, they picked up their bags and left.

It grew dark as the fire went out. The furniture vanished like hills in a mist. Cobwebs decorated the walls once again.

The stem!

Alison looked frantically through the room. The table had disappeared, too.

Bang!

The door crashed open. There stood Jill, wide-eyed. "Let's go!" she shouted. "I'm never coming here again, even if you promise me you'll set the table for a year. This place creeps me out."

"Did you see them?" Alison cried. "Did you see Lucia and her Father? They must have gone right by you."

"I didn't see anything. It's just too spooky." Jill turned and ran.

7

Fathers

Alison didn't catch up with her speeding sister until they were a block from home.

"You took forever," Jill said, angry. "Did you find anything?"

"Not exactly, but I know where it is, sort of, if I ever find — " A fit of sneezes stopped her. "Ugh! The dust in that house!"

On second thought, Alison decided to keep quiet about what had happened. She could tell from the expression on Jill's face that she'd probably think she'd been dreaming again. No, she'd wait until Dad came tomorrow night. He was good at figuring things out. Maybe that way she wouldn't have to go back to the house again.

"Don't tell the others where we've been," Alison said.

"Okay," agreed Jill, who could usually keep a secret.

"When do you think Dad and Uncle Bruce and Grandpa will get here tomorrow?" Alison asked, hoping to change the subject.

"The sooner, the better," Jill said.

The next day everyone helped to vacuum the house, find the roaming socks under the bed and pick bouquets of asters. James was told to gather logs for the fire outside, while Graham helped Grandma make Blueberry Grunt.

They were just gathering up the last stash of Katie's new shells when she called excitedly from the front garden. Uncle Bruce had arrived from Ottawa. He'd driven all day and all night. Then their dad came from Halifax, and finally, Grandpa, back from his fishing trip to New Brunswick.

The first thing Grandpa always did was inspect the grass. Sure enough, he complained loudly to Grandma. "It's an absolute disgrace.

There'll have to be an attack on that jungle you call a garden first thing in the morning." He frowned fiercely and looked around for potential recruits. The grandchildren, of course, all laughed. Whenever Grandpa roared that much, they knew he was happy.

The evening was warm, and they had a big family dinner at the table in the garden under the cherry tree. Grandpa loved eating in the garden even more than cutting the grass. The children interrupted each other to tell of their summer adventures, between bites of scallop chowder, baked beans, brown bread and, of course, Blueberry Grunt for dessert. Grimble lurked under the table hunting for scraps. But the foolish kitten kept sitting on people's feet and finally had to be locked in the house, where he clawed at the screen door, yowling. "Like a banshee," said Grandpa, when he went to let him out.

When it grew dark and bats started flitting silently among the trees, Grandpa lit a fire in the outdoor fireplace he'd built many years ago. They gathered around the burning logs and watched small streams of sparks rise into the night. A slight wind rustled the leaves with a hint of the coming fall, and something small and hunted squealed in the distance.

I hope it isn't Grimble, killing a bird. Just then he jumped onto Alison's lap and began to purr like a small motorboat.

Jill and Katie perched on either side of their father's chair, telling him in great detail about their finds at the Starry, Starry Night Sale.

"What did *you* find?" her father asked Alison. "Any special treasure?"

"I didn't buy anything, but Captain Entwhistle gave me a present." She reached into her pocket, pulled out the pipe bowl and handed it to her father. The grey stone glowed as he held it close to the firelight to inspect the designs.

"This could be very old. Definitely Mi'kmaq work. It would have had a wooden stem to fit into this hole. I wonder if it still smokes well?"

He rummaged through his pockets, producing a small knife, pen, car keys, change and two of his own pipes. He removed the stem from one and tried it, but it wouldn't fit.

Alison watched anxiously as her father fiddled with the pipe.

"Aha!" he exclaimed as the stem from the second pipe slid into the small hole at the base of the stone. He examined it, smiling his approval. Then he began filling it with tobacco.

Alison held her breath.

Maybe I should warn him. What if something happens and he's whirled back to the past?

Her father lit the pipe with a glowing splinter of wood from the fire.

"Isn't it your bedtime, Katie?" he asked, drawing on the pipe and puffing out a fragrant cloud of smoke.

Katie frowned. "Do I have to? Tell us a story first, please!"

"Well, maybe just a short one. Let me think." He puffed on the pipe for a moment. Alison watched him, worrying.

"Many years ago," he began, "not far from here, there lived a young shaman who was a powerful healer. He had travelled widely throughout the land learning from the wisest of the other shamans." As he spoke, their dad's voice grew deeper and deeper as though coming from far away through the smoke.

"Winter was near and the animals were plentiful, but there was almost no one left in the band healthy enough to hunt. A strange sickness was killing the people. The shaman worked day and night, trying every cure he knew: plants, potions, sacred dances, but nothing he did helped. Then he, too, caught the disease. For six days, his fever raged and only the constant care of an old woman kept him alive. Late one night his fever broke and he began a slow recovery.

"When he was strong enough to walk again, he put on his cloak of beaver fur and his winged headband, planning to return to his battle against the disease that had killed so many of his people.

"It was then that he discovered his pipe was missing. He needed the pipe because its sacred smoke had strong medicine. But it could also harm those who did not understand its powers.

"The shaman searched his wigwam and the

woods nearby, where he had first been struck by the fever, but he never found it."

A shiver ran down Alison's spine. All eyes were on her father as he continued his story.

"He did his best to help the sick, still using the old cures, until finally the disease had run its course and there were no new sick people. The winter that followed was long and hard, for there were few men left strong enough to hunt. Eventually the arrival of spring brought health and strength back to the band.

"The shaman grew wiser and he served his people well. But he was haunted by the loss of his pipe. His search continued, becoming more desperate through the years, for he knew that without it, he could not rest in the spirit world."

The fire had died down, and Alison's father stopped to put on another log. As he bent down close to the flames, the flickering light painted red, then black lines on his face.

Alison squeezed her eyes shut as fear burned inside her.

"Years passed," her father said, taking up his

story again. "The shaman continued his lonely quest. He roams in spirit still, his bones long since turned to dust. He is always watching, always waiting.

"In its dangerous wanderings, the pipe had come at last to a man who lived not far from here. It brought pain and suffering to him too. His wife died suddenly, his crops failed. But perhaps the powers of the pipe were dwindling, or perhaps he was a better man than those who had held it before. Whatever the reason, he found the strength to fight the pipe's strange power, for he feared for the safety of his young daughter.

"Then one day — "

He stopped suddenly and tapped the ash from the pipe into the fire. "That's enough for tonight. Time for bed, everyone." He removed his stem from the bowl and handed it back to Alison. It was still warm in her hand.

"Smokes well," he said to her, "but it has a slightly bitter taste." Alison was relieved. Dad's voice was back to normal.

"You can't stop there, Daddy," Katie objected.

"Where's the happy ending?"

"I need more time to remember it," he said, laughing. "Maybe tomorrow night."

But Alison knew the story didn't have an ending. Not yet.

8

A Handful of Sand

"Now let's clean up this barn."

Alison's father surveyed the jumble of furniture, trunks and cardboard boxes that looked ready to fall out the door. She hadn't had a chance yet to ask him about the story he didn't finish last night. Maybe this afternoon she could get him alone and tell him her part of the story.

James, Graham and Jill were already busy cleaning up the playhouse, which had been mostly used this summer by Katie and Grimble for frequent tea parties.

Her Father and Uncle Bruce began heaving monstrous chests and tables about. This was an annual ritual as they decided which of the summer's purchases would fit into the cars with the rest of the luggage to be taken home. Of course, they also had to leave room for seashell collections, precious rocks and works of art. Alison went in to enjoy the confusion.

"Ugh. Would you look at that?" said her father. He had uncovered a hideous Victorian chair. They stared at it, hypnotized by its ugliness. Uncle Bruce sat down and twined his arms through its carved arms like a six-foot spider.

"Mother bought it at an auction," said Alison, "because she felt sorry for it." Her father looked desperate.

"Isn't it wonderful?" Her mother stood in the doorway.

"Utterly unique," said Uncle Bruce, chuckling as Alison's father dragged it out from the wall.

"I suppose this pile of firewood is yours too?" her father asked as he lifted something from the floor behind the chair.

"Be careful," said her mother. "That's fragile. It's a genuine twig table. I was so lucky to find it that time we went to the flea market in Yarmouth."

Alison and her father stared at the small table, Alison with joyful disbelief, her father in despair.

"I think I could use a cup of coffee," he said at last, and set the table down carefully.

"Me too," said Uncle Bruce, trying hard not to laugh.

Alison waited until the adults had gone off to the house. Then she rushed to the table and carried it into better light. *Is it the same one? Oh, please let it be.*

Dropping to her knees, she ran her hand to the spot where Lucia's father had hidden the stem so many years ago. Had it fallen out? Her fingers searched among the twigs. Where was it? Gone?

No! It was there! She was so excited she had to stop to keep her hands from shaking. Gently, carefully, Alison wiggled the stem back and forth like a loose tooth. And then it was out.

She had it at last!

Looking around, Alison made sure no adults or cousins were coming. Slowly, she pulled the stone from her pocket. Gently she pushed the stem into the small hole at the base of the stone.

83

It went in!

The two parts fitted together perfectly. Alison started breathing again. "It really is beautiful," she said, admiring the graceful curve of the long stem, the pleasing smooth shape of the bowl. "I should find a soft cloth and polish it."

Hiding the completed pipe under her sweater, she went quietly into the house and up to her bedroom. Grimble was there, fast asleep in a purring mound under her quilt. She selected one of her soft wool socks and began to rub the stem. Gradually, the wood began to shine.

Grimble woke up and scrambled out from under the quilt. Interested as always in his family's activities, he stretched out a paw to investigate.

"Get away, you silly cat." Alison pushed him aside more roughly than she intended. He rolled off the bed and landed on the floor with a thump. He howled and hid behind the door.

"It's your own fault, Grimble," she told him. "You shouldn't be so curious."

Alison finished her polishing, then sat staring

at the gleaming wood and stone. *What will happen now?* she wondered. *Will the pipe take me back to the wigwam?* Otherwise, how could she give it back to the shaman?

But maybe she shouldn't try to return it too soon. There was no need to rush. The shaman had been searching for centuries. *Maybe I should keep it a little longer. After all, I was the one who kept looking for it — and found it.*

"What are you doing?"

Katie clunked into the room wearing Grandpa's old lumber boots.

"Nothing." She slid the pipe under the pillow. "Don't bother me. Can't you see I'm busy?"

"How can you be busy if you're doing nothing?"

Alison didn't even try to answer this four-year-old logic. "I'm going outside," she said. "Stay out of my room."

Jill and the boys were in the front garden, gathered around the family fleet of bicycles.

"We're going down to the shore to gather driftwood for the bonfire tonight," Jill said. "Are you coming?"

"You go on ahead. I'll be there in a minute." Alison was suddenly afraid Katie might find the pipe in her bedroom. "She'd probably break it," Alison muttered to herself. "She gets into everything."

The bedroom was empty. Katie and Grimble were in the living room playing their version of paper dolls. As fast as Katie cut them out, Grimble ripped them up. Alison was reluctant to leave the pipe behind, even to go to the shore. It was harder to carry now with its long stem, so she hid it in the inside pocket of her jacket. She soon caught up with the others, but didn't tell them that she'd found the stem. *I'm the only one who really believed in it*, she told herself. *So I'm the only one who deserves to know about it.*

After making a giant stack of driftwood for the evening bonfire, the cousins were pedalling home when they met Captain Entwhistle.

"Well, hello. How are you all?" he asked. "Your family has invited me to join you tonight. I'm just on my way to the store to stock up on marshmallows. I love toasted marshmallows."

"Great!" cried the cousins. They were all fond

of the old sailor. "See you later." Then they tore along the road on their bikes. Captain Entwhistle held up a hand to Alison as the others went ahead. "Have you found that stem yet?"

Startled by the question, she almost fell off the bike. "No," she answered quickly. Avoiding his eyes, she hurried after the others. Her cheeks were burning.

Oh that was so awful. Why did I tell a lie?

Telling the truth was expected of everyone in her family. Alison felt guilty all afternoon and didn't feel like talking to anyone. She didn't tell her father about the pipe or ask him to finish the unfinished story either.

"Alison's sick, Mom," Alison heard Jill say from the kitchen. Jill and the boys were making a ruckus while packing hot dogs, mustard, relish and Mrs. MacLeod's rolls into a cooler to take to the shore. "She's lying down in your room."

"Oh no!" her mother said. "She can't be sick now. We leave for home on Labour Day." She came up to the bedroom to find Alison flopped on the bed.

"What's wrong, dear? Do you have a fever?"

"I just don't feel well. You go ahead without me."

Her father came in and placed the palm of his hand on her forehead. "No fever," he said. "Any pain?"

Alison shook her head.

"I don't know what it is then," he said. "Maybe you're allergic to the thought of going back to school."

That brought only the smallest smile.

"We have to leave now to start the fire before the sun sets," said her mother. "Maybe you'll be well enough to come down later. Grandma and Grandpa are staying here. Call them if you need anything, or if you feel worse."

Noisily, happily, her family set off for the shore, leaving Grandma and Grandpa to enjoy a quiet supper for two under the cherry tree. Upstairs in her room, Alison felt completely miserable.

What's wrong with me? she asked herself. *I'm not sick and I love bonfires. Why am I being a grouch and lying to everyone?* She started to cry, and buried her face in the pillow to muffle her sobs. Her hand bumped against the pipe. She pulled it out and glared at it.

It's all your fault!

There was a loud jingling of brass bells at the front door, and then voices. Grandma called to her from the steps.

"Alison? Captain Entwhistle's here. He heard you were ill, but he wondered if you felt better now, and might like to walk down with him. He says he has too many marshmallows to carry by himself."

Alison wanted to say yes, but something small and unpleasant that had been struggling inside her all day said no. When she heard Captain Entwhistle tramping up the stairs, she quickly slipped the pipe back under her pillow.

"Seems a shame to miss the last bonfire of the season," he said from the doorway. "But if you really feel sick, of course you mustn't go. It's wise of you to be careful. Not many children your age would be so wise." As Captain Entwhistle spoke, he looked slowly around the room. "Why, I remember only last year when you claimed you were perfectly well and able to go to the blueberry festival, yet you were so covered with chicken pox that you looked like one big spot."

He stopped and stared hard at Alison. Or was it at her pillow? "Are you sure you aren't just tired? Perhaps you feel stronger now after your rest. Sometimes I feel quite dizzy after smoking my pipe, but after a short nap I feel full of beans again."

Alison's face burned with shame and guilt. "I found the stem," she blurted out.

Captain Entwhistle smiled. "I thought as much."

Alison felt better at once. She didn't know why she'd admitted it. Perhaps it was to make up for the lie she'd told him earlier. The hard lump of misery that had been stuck in the pit of her stomach all day began to dissolve. "I think maybe I will go after all."

She sat up and grabbed her heavy sweater at the foot of the bed.

"I'll wait for you outside," the Captain said.

She dressed quickly. Before leaving the room, she slid the pipe inside her sweater. "How did you know I'd found the stem?" she asked Captain Entwhistle as they walked along the road to the shore. The ferns were starting to turn brown among a few last sprays of goldenrod.

"When I saw you this morning, you acted strangely," he replied. "You wouldn't look me in the eye when I asked you about the pipe, and then tonight you were suddenly sick. To be sick for a bonfire is most unusual."

"Ever since I found the other part of the pipe, I haven't felt like myself at all," Alison said. It felt so good to finally talk about it.

"What have you felt like?" he asked.

"I haven't liked people," she told him. "I've felt as if I were better than they were and knew best. Then I just wanted to be by myself." She felt a cold chill. "Do you think the pipe's powers could be working on me?"

"They could be."

"How do you know so much about this?" she

asked, suddenly curious.

"Just bits of old stories handed down in the family, but enough to be worried about you this morning. I never thought you'd really find the stem, otherwise I wouldn't have given you the bowl. I guess I forgot to mention that Lucia Mackenzie was my great-grandmother," he added, looking sideways at Alison.

Alison was quiet for a moment. "Did she have a happy life?"

"She certainly did," smiled the Captain. "She married a fine man she met in Ontario. They set up a successful flour-milling business and had eight healthy children."

What a relief! Alison was confused but happy. Somehow, through a time-travelling magic she didn't understand, she had helped Lucia and her father escape. Alison hadn't known that a person could feel so miserable and then so happy all in one day. "I don't suppose you knew her?" she asked.

"Indeed I did. She must have looked a bit like you," he said, thinking about it. "Brown hair and green eyes she had as a girl, my mother told me. Of course Granny was ninety-five when I knew her. Lively as a cricket even then. She told me many strange tales, although she could never bring herself to tell me the whole story of the pipe. Said she was still afraid of it. That left me curious. When I moved back here to live, I went poking about in the old house to see what I could find."

"And you found the bowl," Alison said. "Now I have the whole pipe. But I don't want to keep it if it makes me as mean as I've been today. I want to get rid of it quickly."

"I'll take it if you like," offered Captain Entwhistle. "I'd never forgive myself if anything happened to you or your family. I'd hold myself responsible because I gave you the bowl in the first place and started you on this search."

"No," Alison said. "Why should you get in trouble?" She couldn't bear to think of friendly Captain Entwhistle turning mean. "I know who needs the pipe, but I don't know how to get it to him. I only hope I see him soon. I'm sure he's looking for me."

"Well, let me know if I can help," Captain Entwhistle said as they reached the shore.

"Alison, I'm glad you made it." Uncle Bruce greeted her with a smile as he threw a big log on the fire.

"Feeling better?" her father asked. "Be sure you don't get a chill. The air is cold when the sun goes down."

Katie was clambering on a log near the edge of the water, while Jill and the boys chased each other, throwing hard little green apples.

"Perfect timing, Alison," Aunt Karin said. "Supper, everyone! Come and get it!"

Everyone agreed that there had never been such a meal. The hot dogs were fat and juicy, and Mrs. MacLeod had never made such a splendid batch of rolls.

Later, Alison toasted several marshmallows for Captain Entwhistle until they were just right: crispy golden-brown outside and a molten-white sweetness within. The Captain seemed to have forgotten all about the pipe. He told Alison a rambling story about a wolf chasing his great-

great-grandmother through the woods while she carried her baby in her arms.

"And lucky for me, she escaped," he said, laughing, "or I wouldn't be here today eating this magnificent marshmallow."

Afterwards, well-fed and at peace, everyone sat around the fire and sang songs. Captain Entwhistle taught them several lively sea shanties about pirates, and mermaids and great whales. A full moon hung low in the sky, and its silvery path rippled across the bay. Katie stirred in her mother's lap. She and Graham had been having a marshmallow-eating contest, but now all Captain Entwhistle's bags were empty. "Finish the story, Daddy," Katie said, with a yawn.

"Which one?" her father asked, staring into the fire.

"You know, the sad one about the shaman you told last night."

"I don't remember any story about a shaman. You must have been half-asleep." He threw more wood on the fire and stared at the leaping flames as if hypnotized.

He's forgotten!

"You must remember!" Katie insisted.

"Did I ever tell you about 'Cluny's Treasure?'" he asked, trying to change the subject.

Katie shook her head. "Nope."

"Will that do instead?"

She nodded and settled down under her blanket.

"Seven stones stood by the water's edge … "

Alison wasn't in the mood for a story. She felt like being alone again, but this time it was a friendly feeling. She wasn't mad at anyone, or ready to bite their heads off if they spoke to her. She just wanted to be by herself for a while to think about the magic that had happened to her. What a summer it had been, with games and adventures — and magic, scary and exciting.

Quietly, so as not to disturb the others, Alison crept away from the fire and wandered down to the edge of the water. She gazed out along the glimmering path of moonlight. There was something out there, a dark shape floating far out in the bay. She looked hard at the object silhouetted against the light. As it came closer,

Alison realized what it was.

A canoe!

A wet paddle flashed as, silently, the canoe came closer and closer. Alison was sure it was a man who was paddling. And he was alone. The birchbark canoe glided into the shallow water and landed with a small crunch on the pebbled beach. The paddler stepped ashore. In the moonlight, she could see the feathers flaring from the sides of his head like the wings of a bird, the long cloak made of many furs.

Yes, it's him.

The shaman stood in front of her, waiting for her to speak.

After all that had happened this summer, Alison was no longer surprised at the things that had gone on. She was grateful, even though she'd been frightened at first.

"I have the pipe," she said.

She thought of the power the pipe had had over her during that long miserable day and shuddered. What would it be like to live under its dreadful spell for days, for the rest of your life?

She pulled the pipe out from her sweater and placed it carefully in his outstretched hand. "There, it's done."

She waited. Would there be flashing lightning and thunder? Would the pipe and shaman both vanish in a puff of smoke?

For the first time, the shaman smiled. He turned the pipe over slowly in his hands. Then he placed it in his pouch. He spoke, but Alison didn't understand his words. He reached into his pouch again, pulled out a bracelet and handed it to Alison. The leather was decorated with coloured porcupine quills, shells and purple and white beads in an intricate pattern, just like the Mi'kmaq work she had seen in the museum.

Alison looked up to thank the shaman, but he was already back in the canoe, gliding away as quickly and silently as he had come.

She stood very still, watching the swift movement of the canoe, etched against the moonlit path. Soon, it was just a black speck on the water again. And then it was gone.

Alison let out a huge sigh. She hoped the

shaman could rest at last, that the pipe would no longer destroy peoples' lives, but heal them. But she felt sad too. The summer was truly over.

"Amazing," she said, out loud.

"Talking to yourself again?"

Jill and James had come down to tell her everyone was ready to go home. "What did you find?" Jill asked, looking at her hand.

"It's a — " Alison looked at her palm. The bracelet had crumbled into sand. Among the grains there were purple and white beads.

"These are neat," Jill said. "Where do you think they came from? A shipwreck?"

"I'm not sure," said Alison, "but I think I'll keep them to remind me of this summer."

They ran to catch up with the others and everyone walked the road home together.

"Is everything all right?" asked Captain Entwhistle.

"Much better than that," Alison said with a smile. "Now I have stories to tell my grandchildren." She looked sideways at the Captain. "Just like the stories Lucia told you!"

Alison stopped to look back across the bay. Something tiny and black floated far out on the silvery water. Was it the shaman? Or only a wave? She wanted to think it was the shaman, at peace at last.